The Duchess of Whimsy

invites you to a soirée

—a most unusual party—

with some most unusual guests

Randall de Sève

Peter de Sève

THE

UCHESS OF

Whimsy

An Absolutely

Delicious Fairy Tale

Philomel Books · Penguin Young Readers Group

The Duchess of Whimsy was known throughout the land for her extravagant soirées, her elaborate attire, her uncommon conversation and her most peculiar pets and acquaintances.

To the Duchess, the Earl of Norm
was as normal as they come.
He wore ordinary clothes,
walked an ordinary dog
and discussed, with great seriousness,
ordinary things—
the kingdom's rutted roads,
the manor's nesting birds
and the rain, or lack thereof—
even if nobody was listening.

The Duchess was the life of the party.
The Earl was . . . well,
let's just say that merrymaking
carried on in spite of him.

Why was the Earl even at the Duchess' soirées?
Because her father, the King, made her invite
him—their kingdoms needed to be friends—
and because the Earl loved the Duchess.
He loved her lively stories.
He loved her wild apparel.
Simply put, he loved her *joie de vivre*.

The Earl of Norm went to absurd lengths
to impress the Duchess of Whimsy.

One evening, he took to her party
a giraffe borrowed from the royal zoo.
It ate the foliage off all the ladies' hats
and had a go at the drawing room wallpaper . . .
before the manor's pest control staff stepped in.

The Earl of Norm composed sugary poetry
comparing the Duchess to
a squid,
a platypus
and a penguin,
and recited it before an astounded audience
of giggling guests.

The Earl even went so far as to arrive one evening
in a brightly brocaded cape
borrowed from his flamboyant twin brother, Nigel.
It did not suit him at all.

The Duchess of Whimsy could not bear
the Earl's silly attempts to win her attention.
"Still too *ordinary*!" she said to her father.
"Our kingdoms need to be friends," said the King.

One evening, the Duchess of Whimsy
invited her usual guests for supper
when suddenly Cook took ill.
Panic reigned.
What were they all to eat?
Out came the cookbooks.
Out came the chef hats.
Out came the giant bowls and spoons,
and everyone swung into action.

The Marquise of Charisma made truffle canapés.
But first she had to sniff out truffles in the forest—
with a pig.

The Shah of Huzzah made a watercress salad
with pickled quail eggs.
But first he had to find the quail
and snatch its eggs.

The Duke of Dreams made a velvet midnight cake
topped with an entire galaxy of spun sugar stars.
But first he had to learn how to spin sugar.

The Earl of Norm had no knack for cooking
and, by now, no desire to try.
So he whipped up the only thing he knew how—
a grilled cheese sandwich and a glass of milk—
and sat down quietly to eat.

Figures, thought the Duchess.

But then she took another look at his plate.

His sandwich looked so scrumptious.

His milk looked so refreshing.

How could something so *ordinary* look so good?

The Earl noticed the Duchess
staring at his sandwich
and, of course, he offered her a bite.

For a moment, she studied the sandwich—
its golden, crusty bread,
its glistening, melted cheese—
then, without further delay, she took the bite.

It was
delicious!
It was
delectable!

It was *Divine*!!

Then, while her other guests
were still toiling away in the kitchen,
the Duchess of Whimsy and
the Earl of Norm got to talking.

It turned out the Earl could actually tell a good joke.

He liked bright colors and was eager to learn how to wear them.

His dog he had even bravely rescued from a traveling circus!

It turned out the Duchess liked quiet walks in the woods
and sitting by the frog pond alone at twilight.

She especially liked to hear spring peepers sing.

Once the Earl got to know the Duchess, he liked her even more.

Once the Duchess got to know the Earl, she rather liked him too.

Together, that night,
the Earl and the Duchess enjoyed
the sumptuous feast finally
laid out by her exhausted guests.

*A*nd forever after they spent
their evenings together
enjoying each other.
It turned out the Duchess of Whimsy
and the Earl of Norm found each other to be . . .
simply extraordinary!

For the original

Duchess of Whimsy

and Earl of Norm.

With love,

R&P

Patricia Lee Gauch, Editor

PHILOMEL BOOKS
A division of Penguin Young Readers Group.
Published by The Penguin Group.
Penguin Group (USA) Inc., 375 Hudson Street, New York, NY 10014, U.S.A.
Penguin Group (Canada), 90 Eglinton Avenue East, Suite 700, Toronto, Ontario M4P 2Y3, Canada (a division of Pearson Penguin Canada Inc.).
Penguin Books Ltd, 80 Strand, London WC2R 0RL, England.
Penguin Ireland, 25 St. Stephen's Green, Dublin 2, Ireland (a division of Penguin Books Ltd).
Penguin Group (Australia), 250 Camberwell Road, Camberwell, Victoria 3124, Australia (a division of Pearson Australia Group Pty Ltd).
Penguin Books India Pvt Ltd, 11 Community Centre, Panchsheel Park, New Delhi - 110 017, India.
Penguin Group (NZ), 67 Apollo Drive, Rosedale, North Shore 0632, New Zealand (a division of Pearson New Zealand Ltd).
Penguin Books (South Africa) (Pty) Ltd, 24 Sturdee Avenue, Rosebank, Johannesburg 2196, South Africa.
Penguin Books Ltd, Registered Offices: 80 Strand, London WC2R 0RL, England.

Text copyright © 2009 by Randall de Sève. Illustrations copyright © 2009 by Peter de Sève.
All rights reserved. This book, or parts thereof, may not be reproduced in any form without permission in writing from the publisher, Philomel Books, a division of Penguin Young Readers Group, 345 Hudson Street, New York, NY 10014. Philomel Books, Reg. U.S. Pat. & Tm. Off. The scanning, uploading and distribution of this book via the Internet or via any other means without the permission of the publisher is illegal and punishable by law. Please purchase only authorized electronic editions, and do not participate in or encourage electronic piracy of copyrighted materials. Your support of the author's rights is appreciated. The publisher does not have any control over and does not assume any responsibility for author or third-party websites or their content.
Published simultaneously in Canada.
Manufactured in China by South China Printing Co. Ltd.
Design by Semadar Megged.
Library of Congress Cataloging-in-Publication Data is available upon request.

ISBN 978-0-399-25095-8
3 5 7 9 10 8 6 4